Dedicated to all the kids
who barely tidy their room.
Big bear hugs to
Genevieve and Alison.

First U.S. edition 2018

Library of Congress Catalog Card Number pending
ISBN 978-0-7636-9646-7

TLF 22 21 20 19 18 17
10 9 8 7 6 5 4 3 2 1

Printed in Dongguan, Guangdong, China

This book was typeset in Adobe Caslon.
The illustrations were created digitally.

TEMPLAR BOOKS

an imprint of
Candlewick Press
99 Dover Street
Somerville, Massachusetts 02144
www.candlewick.com

YUVAL ZOMMER

Big Brown Bear's Cave

templar books

an imprint of Candlewick Press

One day, Big Brown Bear was strolling
in the forest when he saw a cave.
It was dark and dusty and just right
for a bear like him.

"What luck!" Big Brown Bear said with a grin.

He moved in right away.

That night he bear-stretched on one side of the cave . . .

then in the middle . . .

then on the **other side.**

But no matter where he tried, the cave just didn't fit quite **right.**

So Big Brown Bear went for another stroll.

At the edge of the forest, he discovered
something very interesting indeed.

Humans had their own caves!

The human caves were dark
and dusty, just like Bear's.
But they weren't empty.

They were full of STUFF!

There was stuff on the floor,
stuff on shelves, stuff
in boxes. . . .

"I need stuff, too!"
said Big Brown Bear.
"Then I'll have the
perfect cave."

So Bear decided to gather some STUFF for himself.

There was all kinds of stuff to choose from,
but Bear's favorites were:

stuff that came
with wheels,

stuff that came
with handles,

and stuff that
came in boxes.

"I won't stop until I fill every corner of my cave," said Bear.

"My cave will have the most stuff ever!"

Word spread about Big Brown Bear's cave.

"May we come in?" asked his friends.

"I'm sorry," said Big Brown Bear.

"There's not enough room for visitors."

Pretty soon there was no room
left in the cave to even stretch or
scratch or do any of the other things
that bears generally like to do.

Later, Big Brown Bear's friends asked,

"Won't you join us for a fishing trip?"

"I'm sorry," said Big Brown Bear, tumbling

headfirst into the stuff. "But I seem to be . . .

Bear's friends tried pulling him from one side . . .

then they tried pulling him from the middle.

Next they tried pulling him from the other side . . .

until POP! at last he was free.

Bear and his friends decided to take all the **stuff** back to the humans' caves.

At last Bear's cave was empty again.

But with his **friends** beside him,
Bear found the perfect spot for sleeping
right away.

Finally, his cave felt like home.